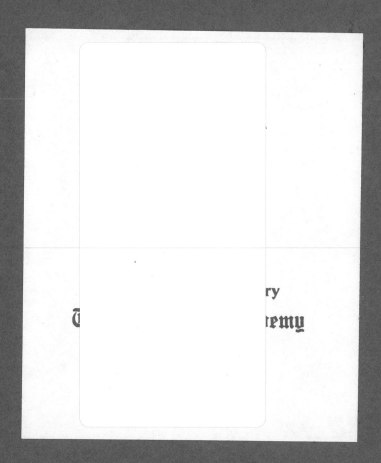

ry

T   emy

T.H.E SUNDAY OUTING

by GLORIA JEAN PINKNEY · *pictures by* JERRY PINKNEY

Dial Books for Young Readers   *New York*

Published by Dial Books for Young Readers
A Division of Penguin Books USA Inc.
375 Hudson Street
New York, New York 10014
Text copyright © 1994 by Gloria Jean Pinkney
Pictures copyright © 1994 by Jerry Pinkney
All rights reserved
Typography by Jane Byers Bierhorst
Printed in the U.S.A.
First Edition
1   3   5   7   9   10   8   6   4   2

Library of Congress Cataloging in Publication Data

Pinkney, Gloria Jean
The Sunday outing : by Gloria Jean Pinkney
pictures by Jerry Pinkney
p.   cm.
Summary : Ernestine, who loves going to the
railroad station and watching the trains come and go,
finally realizes her dream of going on a train trip
south to visit family.
ISBN 0-8037-1198-0 (trade)—ISBN 0-8037-1199-9 (library)
[1. Railroads—Fiction.   2. Afro-Americans—Fiction.]
I. Pinkney, Jerry, ill.   II. Title.
PZ7.P8334Su   1994   [E]—dc20   93-25383   CIP   AC

The full-color artwork was prepared using pencil,
colored pencils, and watercolor.
It was then color-separated and reproduced as
red, blue, yellow, and black halftones.

"Mama, what time is it?" called Ernestine from the front stoop. She had a clear view of the corner, and there wasn't a trolley car in sight. "Aunt Odessa promised to be here right after church."

"It's half past two," answered Mama from the third floor window.

"But, Mama," cried Ernestine, "I'm going to miss seeing the North Carolina train!"

Just then Buddy Lee, May, and Bell came up the block. "V.K. has colored chalks," said Buddy Lee. "We're going to draw a hop-scotch. Want to come?"

Ernestine shook her head. "I can't today. I'm going to the railroad station!"

"Again?!" Bell said. "Let's go, Buddy Lee. Come on, May. We'll get Jeanette. Anyway, Ernestine Avery Powell, what's the point in going to watch those ole trains? You're never going to ride one."

Ernestine covered her ears with her hands. "How would you know, Bell Edwards!"

Ernestine loved going to North Philadelphia Station with her great-aunt Odessa Powell on warm summer Sundays and listening to stories about Great-uncle Ariah who had worked for the railroad. Best of all Ernestine could see the trains going south and imagine herself riding one to Lumberton, the town in North Carolina where she was born.

She watched her friends playing hopscotch for a while, then jumped down from the stoop. "I *will* ride one someday," she called out to them.

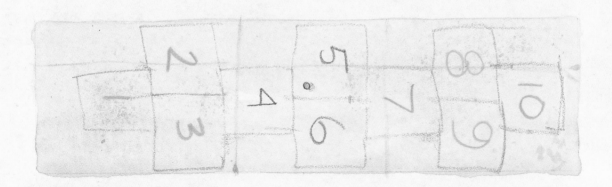

Right then a trolley car stopped at the corner. "Mama," Ernestine shouted, "Aunt Odessa's here."

Aunt Odessa Powell was walking down Sixteenth Street, swinging her large black handbag in one hand and moving the other hand with her own bouncy rhythm. Ernestine ran to greet her great-aunt. "Afternoon, youngun," she said, hugging her niece. "Sorry I'm late. You wasn't worried now, was you?"

"I wasn't *really* worried," Ernestine said, looking down at the sidewalk.

Aunt Odessa waved to Mama, then said, "Youngun, run down to the corner and see if the trolley is coming."

"Good-bye, Mama," Ernestine called. "Hurry, Aunt Odessa. I think I hear it."

"I'm moving as fast as these ole legs will carry me," her aunt said. "Hop on up there and find us seats."

As soon as they sat down, Ernestine closed her eyes and pretended that she was heading south on the Silver Star or the Palmetto.

"You're mighty quiet today," said her aunt. "What's on your mind?"

Ernestine looked up at her aunt. "Mama's people invited me to their farm in Lumberton, but Mama and Daddy said I can't go."

"Your folks must have a good reason for saying so," her aunt responded.

"They said we can't afford a ticket now, because we're saving to buy our own house."

Aunt Odessa was quiet for a moment. "Well," she said, "they've been wanting to move out of that apartment for some time. The way I see it, you'll have to think of something that will save your folks money, so they'll be able to buy that ticket."

A few minutes later the trolley car stopped in front of the railroad station. They could hear the announcement on the loud-speaker: "NOW ARRIVING ON TRACK NUMBER TWO...THE PALMETTO...MAKING STOPS IN DELAWARE...MARYLAND ...WASHINGTON...VIRGINIA...AND THE CAROLINAS...ALL ABOARD!"

"We have to hurry," Ernestine cried as the slow wooden electric stairs carried them up to the platform. She could feel the vibrations, a soft rumbling beneath her feet, then heard a faint sound in the distance, growing louder until at last the Palmetto pulled into the station.

"Come on, youngun, let's find a bench in the shade and eat our sandwiches," Aunt Odessa said, opening her handbag.

Ernestine admired the passengers getting on the Palmetto. Suddenly a little boy on the train waved to her. Ernestine waved back. "He's lucky," she said. Then she thought about Aunt Odessa's advice. But she was baffled.

"Please tell me what I should give up," she said when they rode the trolley car home from the station.

"Give yourself time," her aunt instructed. "You'll think of something."

After dinner Ernestine and Daddy listened to the Sunday Gospel Hour on the radio, while Mama and Aunt Odessa looked through a new mail-order catalog. "These are the fabrics that Ernestine and I selected for her school clothes," said Mama.

Ernestine couldn't believe her ears. "I don't need new school clothes, Mama," she blurted out the second she found her voice.

Daddy switched off the radio. "What's this I hear?" he asked.

"Then we'd have enough for my train ticket, Daddy. Couldn't I have that instead? You all are always talking about down home. I've never been on a farm. I try to imagine it, but I can't. Please say I can go!"

Daddy and Mama looked at each other. At last Mama spoke. "It's past your bedtime, Ernestine," she said gently. "Your daddy and I will discuss this tonight, and we'll talk to you in the morning."

"Well," Aunt Odessa said. "I'm going to mosey on home. Good night, all." Ernestine hugged everyone tightly, then slowly headed for bed.

Mama went over to her sewing machine, and pressed the foot pedal. "We can give up some things too," she said. "I have a little saved for the down payment on that electric sewing machine."

Daddy sat down at his desk and began figuring. "Well," he said, leaning back in his chair, "I can manage at work without a new tool set for a while longer. Then we'll have enough for the fare."

Ernestine was already wide awake when her parents tiptoed into her room early the next day. "Ernestine," Daddy called softly, "you're going to Lumberton on...what's the name of that morning train?"

She jumped right out of bed. "The Silver Star! I can go!" she shouted.

After breakfast she ran outside to tell her friends. They were on V.K.'s stoop, trading marbles.

"You're going all by yourself?" Bell asked.

"Wish I could go with you," May said.

"Hope you don't get lost," Jeanette added.

"She'll be okay," Buddy Lee said. "I rode to Chicago alone. Besides, they give kids an I.D. tag to wear, with your name, where you're going, and who's meeting you."

"Sounds easy," Ernestine said, but suddenly she wasn't so sure.

When Ernestine awoke the next day, she felt as if caterpillars were dancing inside her stomach. She found Mama at her sewing machine. "I really want to go," she said, "but I'm scared."

Mama drew Ernestine close. "I was afraid on my first train ride alone. But we'll explain everything about the trip before you leave. And there will be so much to see, you'll have a wonderful time."

Ernestine had a big smile on her face when Aunt Odessa came by that afternoon. "They said Yes!" she told her aunt, then crinkled up her nose. "But I wish you could come with me. What if I miss my stop?"

"I've traveled far in my day, youngun, and now it's your time. But no need to worry, the conductor will announce the stations. He'll see that you get off."

Suppose I fall asleep and don't hear him, Ernestine thought. She was waiting on the stoop for Daddy when he came home from work. "Who's going to meet me at the station?" Ernestine asked.

"We already sent a telegram to Aunt Beula," Daddy told her, "with the name of your train and the time you'll be arriving."

When the doorbell rang the following day, Ernestine ran down the stairs and opened the door. "It's Western Union!" she called.

Mama read the telegram out loud. "Uncle June and Cousin Jack will meet Ernestine at Robeson County Depot. Love, Aunt Beula."

Ernestine frowned. "But I don't remember what they look like."

Mama took out the family album and they went through it together. "This is Jack when he was about your age," she said. "And here's Aunt Beula, laughing as always."

Ernestine looked closely at another photograph of a tall man working in a flower bed. "That's Uncle June!"

Mama smiled and said, "He'll probably bring you a bouquet from his garden."

Mama went over to the closet and took out a fancy suitcase. "This is my wedding satchel. It's old-fashioned, but I want you to have it."

Ernestine picked up the satchel and kissed Mama. "I'll take real good care of it."

"Just remember," Mama told her, "the conductor will watch out for you on the train. When you get to Lumberton, you'll be with family."

Early the next morning they all took Ernestine to the railroad station. As Daddy was purchasing her ticket, an announcement came over the loudspeaker: "ATTENTION, ALL PASSENGERS.... THE SILVER STAR IS RUNNING HALF AN HOUR LATE!"

"A half an hour!" cried Ernestine.

"Be here before you know it," said Aunt Odessa. "Let's head up to the platform and watch the activities."

Aunt Odessa found an empty bench and sat down. "It sure feels good to be out of that hot apartment," Mama said.

"Reminds me of going to the depot with Uncle Ariah when I was a boy," Daddy said, "watching the freights passing through. We'll join you two again, some Sunday." Ernestine couldn't stop grinning.

"We almost forgot your victuals, youngun," Aunt Odessa said. She took out a boxed lunch from her handbag. "We packed enough to hold you till you get down home."

"Thank you, everybody," Ernestine said, just as another announcement came over the loudspeaker. "The train is coming!" she shouted.

"Remember to drop us a line, youngun," Aunt Odessa said, hugging her niece.

After the passengers got off, Daddy walked right up to the conductor. "This is our Ernestine," he said. "She's getting off at Robeson County."

"Let's find a good place for you to sit," Mama said. She chose a window seat near a young couple and asked them to watch over Ernestine.

Ernestine hugged and kissed Mama and Daddy twice. "Good-bye," she called as they headed toward the exit.

"ALL ABOARD!" the conductor yelled.

Ernestine looked about the great train, too excited to feel scared anymore. Then she looked out of the window and waved happily to her family as the Silver Star began the long journey south.

30027000202777

E
PIN   Pinkney, Gloria
           Jean

           The Sunday outing